RICHARD SCARRY'S
The Great Pie Robbery

Who stole Ma Dog's cherry pies?
Sleuths Sam and Dudley put the
clues together to catch the robbers
and bring them to justice.

RICHARD SCARRY'S
The Great Pie Robbery

STERLING CHILDREN'S BOOKS

New York

Sam Cat and Dudley Pig are detectives.
They find children who get lost.
They catch robbers who steal things.

Brrring!

It was Ma Dog calling.
Something was wrong!
What could it be?

They hopped into their car to find out.

Sam and Dudley hurried to Ma Dog's bakery.
"Where did you ever learn how to drive?" shouted the policeman.

"Some thieves have stolen my pies," said Ma Dog.
Dudley looked through his magnifying glass for clues.
Clues are things like fingerprints that thieves leave behind by mistake.
Clues help detectives find thieves.

"Hmmm. There were two of them. I can tell from their
tracks," said Dudley. "Very fine clues to follow."

"Aha! Look there, Sam! The fingerprint clues go out through that little window," said Dudley. "After them!"

"Please give me a boost," said Dudley.

Ugh! Squinch!

"HELP! I'm stuck, Sam. Do something to get me out!"

"Dudley, LOOK!
There go the thieves," said Sam.

"Aha! One of them has torn his pants on that rosebush," said Dudley.
"Aha! They have left footprint clues in the mud leading to that car.

THERE THEY GO NOW!"

shouted Dudley. "I can tell it is them
because they have cherry pie on their faces!"
Dudley is very good at clues.

"Hurry up, Sam. We mustn't let them get out of our sight," said Dudley.

Through the crowded streets they chased the robbers.

"Dudley," said Sam, "maybe we should let that big truck come through the tunnel first."

"Oh, I can see that there is plenty of room for both of us," said Dudley.

Crrrunch!

"Now, wouldn't you think that truck driver could have seen that there wasn't enough room for both of us?" said Dudley. "I wonder where he ever learned how to drive?"

"Come on, Sam. Hurry! We must catch the thieves," said Dudley.

Sam and Dudley needed a new car to chase after the robbers.
Dudley stopped a car.
"My dear lady," he said. "Please follow that car."
The lady did as she was asked.

The robbers ran into the restaurant.
"Follow them!" said Dudley.
The lady followed them.

The waiter asked them what they wanted.
"Two thieves with cherry pie on their faces," said Dudley.

"I don't know if we have any thieves,"
said the waiter, "but we do have all kinds of other
people who have cherry pie on their faces."

Dudley was puzzled.
How would he ever be able to tell the two
cherry pie thieves from the others?

"I have a plan," said Sam. "One of the thieves tore his pants on the rosebush. If we find a pair of torn pants, there will probably be a thief in them."
"But we can't see torn pants if the thieves are sitting down," said Dudley. "How will we get them to stand up?"

Sam whispered the rest of the plan into Dudley's ear.
"You are a smart planner, Sam," said Dudley. "Let's try it."

Dudley went to a table and asked, "Pardon me, but is either one of you gentlemen sitting on my hat?"

The two gentlemen stood up to see if they were. Sam looked for holes in their pants. No! They weren't the thieves.

Then Dudley asked Wart Hog and Baboon if they were sitting on his hat.
"No, we are sitting on our own hats," said Wart Hog.

They stood up to show him.
Sam saw that they did not have torn pants.
They were not the thieves.

They then went to another table.
"Pardon me," said Dudley again. "Are you sitting—"

Horace Wolf and Croaky Crocodile leaped out of their chairs!
Croaky was wearing torn pants!

AHA!

THE THIEVES!

Before Sam and Dudley could do anything, Horace Wolf
threw the tablecloth over their heads!

Hurry up, Sam!
Hurry up, Dudley!

Don't let the thieves get away now!
You almost had them!

While Sam and Dudley struggled to get
out of the tablecloth, the thieves ran away.

The thieves jumped onto a trolley car that was passing by.

Dudley caught the trolley car just in time.
Sam caught Dudley just in time.

Then all of a sudden the trolley stopped. Horace and Croaky ran into their house.
It had strong bars on the windows and doors to keep everyone out.
Now Sam and Dudley had to think of a way to make the thieves come out.

"I have an idea," said Sam.
Dudley listened and said,
"That is an excellent plan, Sam.
May I be on top?"

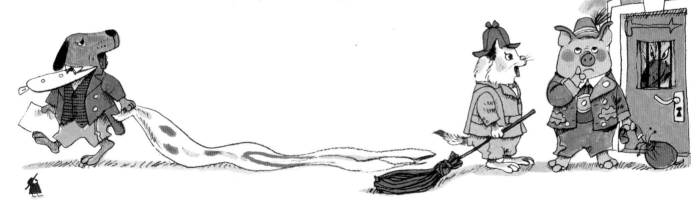

Sam and Dudley hid behind a telephone booth. Dudley opened his special umbrella. Why is it a special umbrella? Because it is full of amazing disguises! There are clothes in his umbrella that can make Sam and Dudley look like ANYTHING!

Dudley put on the top part
of the disguise. Sam dressed
in the bottom part.
Then Dudley sat on Sam's shoulders.

A lady hippopotamus knocked on the thieves' front door.
"What is it?" asked Horace from inside.
"I have a surprise for you," said the lady.
"Come out and see what it is."

Horace and Croaky stepped
out of their house. They did not
see the trap that the lady
hippopotamus had prepared for them.
"Where is our surprise?"
they demanded.

"RIGHT THERE!"

said the lady hippopotamus.
Sam pulled hard on the rope and those two thieves,
Horace Wolf and Croaky Crocodile, were captured!

Sam and Dudley tied their prisoners to the top of a taxi.
They drove back to Ma Dog's bakery.
She would know how to punish a couple of pie stealers!

"You naughty thieves," said Ma Dog.
"For punishment you will have to wash all my pots and pans."

"Oooh!" said Horace and Croaky together.
Maybe THAT will teach them to be good!

And she had an enormous cherry pie for Sam and Dudley.
What a delicious reward!
"Here! Let me carry it, Sam," said Dudley.
"You might drop it. Thank you very much, Ma Dog."

"Oh, dear! Are you all right, Dudley?" asked Sam.

Wasn't it lucky that Ma Dog had another pie to give them?
"You carry it this time," said Dudley.
Ma Dog waved good-bye to the two great detectives.
They had done a fine day's work.

STERLING CHILDREN'S BOOKS
New York

An Imprint of Sterling Publishing
387 Park Avenue South
New York, NY 10016

STERLING CHILDREN'S BOOKS and the distinctive Sterling Children's Books logo
are trademarks of Sterling Publishing Co., Inc.

Published in 2014 by Sterling Publishing Company, Inc.
in association with JB Communications, Inc.
41 River Terrace, New York, New York
Previously published in 2008 by Sterling Publishing Company, Inc., in one volume with two other Richard Scarry titles (*The Supermarket Mystery*
and *The Great Steamboat Mystery*) under the title *The Great Pie Robbery and Other Mysteries* (hardcover)

ISBN 978-1-4549-1009-1

Distributed in Canada by Sterling Publishing
c/o Canadian Manda Group, 165 Dufferin Street
Toronto, Ontario, Canada M6K 3H6
Distributed in the United Kingdom by GMC Distribution Services
Castle Place, 166 High Street, Lewes, East Sussex, England BN7 1XU
Distributed in Australia by Capricorn Link (Australia) Pty. Ltd.
P.O. Box 704, Windsor, NSW 2756, Australia

For information about custom editions, special sales, and premium and corporate purchases,
please contact Sterling Special Sales at 800-805-5489 or specialsales@sterlingpublishing.com.

Printed in China
Lot #:
2 4 6 8 10 9 7 5 3 1
11/13

www.sterlingpublishing.com/kids